Contents

1   The Haunted Valley   1

2   The Wicked Shepherd   7

3   Glam's Return   13

4   The Strongest Man in Iceland   18

5   Staying the Night   22

6   Waiting for Glam   28

7   The Fight   35

8   Victor   43

Battle Cards   48

D0808875

Chapter 1
The Haunted Valley

This is something that happened in Iceland way back. People still talk of it, but rarely after dark.

In the north of the country there was a long, deep valley that ran from the hills down to the sea. In winter the sun never reached the bottom of the valley, so it was called the Shadow Vale. A farmer named Thorhall lived here with his wife and household. He was a rich man who owned a large flock of sheep, but he was unlucky too, because the valley was haunted by a monster.

One day Thorhall went to see a friend of his, Skapti the Lawgiver.

"I need some help, Skapti," he said.

"What's the problem?" asked Skapti.

"I can't find anyone willing to be my shepherd," Thorhall replied, scratching at his beard. "We've had trouble high up in the valley. There's something wicked up there, hiding among the rocks and stones. Men have come back injured, goggle-eyed, scared almost to death. They've packed and left, without a word, and now my sheep are roaming free up on the hill."

Skapti thought for a moment, looking into the fire. "Here's my advice," he said. "See what you think. I know a fellow named Glam. He came here from Sweden last year. I've never met anyone stronger or more stubborn. He won't be put off by talk of ghosts or trolls. He needs a job too, but I warn you that he's not the nicest man around."

"That doesn't bother me," Thorhall said, standing up. "How can I find him?"

"He's up on the hillside, collecting wood," Skapti replied. "You'll know him when you see him."

Thorhall set off up the hill and it wasn't long before he saw a man coming towards him, carrying a huge bundle of twigs and branches. Right away, Thorhall began to wonder whether he should forget his plan, because there was something odd about the look of the stranger. He was almost seven feet tall, with a chest like a beer barrel and great strong arms. His head was huge, with

eyes as dark as slate and a shock of hair streaked grey like a wolf's skin.

The two men stopped and stared at each other.

"I'm looking for someone named Glam," Thorhall began.

The tall man said nothing. His eyes seemed to pierce the farmer through.

"I've a job to offer him," Thorhall went on. "If he wants it, that is."

"My name is Glam," the man said. "And I'm not afraid of work, if my terms are met."

"What are your terms?" Thorhall asked, feeling nervous.

"That no one bothers me," Glam said. He turned and spat on the stones beside him. "I don't like people getting in my way."

"That's fine by me," Thorhall said. "I need a shepherd, but I should tell you that the hill above my farm is haunted."

Glam laughed, showing his teeth. "It'll take more than old wives' tales to put me off," he said. "Anyway, I'd find ghosts better company than most men."

Chapter 2
The Wicked Shepherd

Thorhall struck a bargain with Glam, and he came to live in the household at Shadow Vale. He was a good shepherd, but no one liked him. He was rude and aggressive, and on Sundays he refused to set foot in the church with the rest of the workers. Still, Thorhall didn't mind because Glam seemed to be having no trouble up in the valley.

Winter set in and Christmas came. On Christmas Eve, it was the custom for the

7

household to fast. No one would eat anything out of respect for the holy day to come. But Glam went to Thorhall's wife and sat down at the table.

"Don't give me your nonsense," he said. "I'm hungry and I'll be fed. Get me my breakfast, or you'll regret it."

Thorhall's wife was terrified and brought him some food. Glam ate without another word, then went out, slamming the door behind him.

All that day the weather grew worse. It was pitch black outside and the snow fell thick and fast. The people in Thorhall's farm could hear Glam far off, calling the sheep, but in the afternoon a blizzard set in and his voice was drowned out by the howling wind.

In the evening everyone went to church. When they came back to the farm, walking doubled over against the driving snow, they found that Glam had still not returned. The weather was so bad that no one went to search for him.

The night passed. Glam did not come back.

On Christmas morning, the snow lay thick upon the roof-tops and piled high against the barns and the rocks on the hills. Thorhall's sheep could be seen scattered all across the mountain. After Mass, a search party set out to look for the shepherd. They soon found signs of a titanic battle. Over a wide area the snow had been churned up, rocks had been uprooted and clods of frozen earth had been ripped from the hillside. Splashes of blood were everywhere.

The men crept closer. At last, behind a rock in the centre of the devastation, they found Glam. He was stone dead, with his body

swollen, his skin crusted with ice and his wolfish eyes open, glaring at the sky.

All around Glam's body were huge footprints wider than a man's chest. They led off up the valley, alongside a trail of blood. It was clear to everyone that Glam must have fought with the monster that haunted the valley, and that he had wounded it.

Thorhall's men took hold of the massive body and tried to drag it down to the church. But the corpse was so heavy that no one could shift it, and even when they brought some oxen and tied Glam's feet to the harness they were unable to pull him very far.

The next day, a priest came out with the men to perform a burial service up on the hill. Oddly, while the priest was with the group, Glam could not be found, no matter how hard anyone looked. In the end, the priest returned to the church, and no sooner had he gone than the body was found again. After this, everyone was keener than ever to get rid of the unholy corpse, so without wasting time they buried Glam under a great heap of stones and went away.

Chapter 3
Glam's Return

Perhaps Glam gave the monster of the valley its death wound, because it was never heard of again. But it wasn't long before a much greater evil began to trouble the farm. One night, people came running to Thorhall in terror.

"We've seen him!" they cried. "Walking in the fields! He's come back!"

"Who?" Thorhall asked.

"There's no mistake!" they said. "It's him! We saw his eyes shining, heard his teeth snapping in the dark. He's prowling round the farm, looking for a way in!"

"Who?" Thorhall shouted, although he knew only too well.

"I saw his face in the light of the window!" one man said. "Blue with cold and crazed with hunger. I saw him – Glam!"

"Glam's dead," Thorhall spat.

"He's dead all right," they said. "But he's come back."

That was when the haunting began. Every night, all through the winter, Glam appeared at the farm. He walked among the buildings, knocking on the walls, peering through windows and pushing on doors until the people inside heard the wood crack. He climbed onto the roof and sat there, banging

his heels so hard against the turf that the whole place shook.

Soon, Glam began to appear during the short, dark mid-winter days too. People were terrified. Some fainted, some went mad and others left the valley altogether. These were hard times for Thorhall and his family.

In spring, the hauntings lessened and things were quiet over the summer. But the following winter, Glam returned. His visits grew more frequent and became more violent. Things came to a head on Christmas Eve, a year to the day after Glam had died. Thorhall's new shepherd, a man named Erlend, was about to go out to tend to the sheep when Thorhall's wife stopped him.

"Please don't go," she said. "Stay inside with us. I fear that bad things may repeat themselves today."

Erlend laughed. "It would have to be something pretty dramatic to stop me coming back," he said. "Don't worry yourself. I shall see you later in church."

So Erlend went out, and Erlend did not come back. They found him the next day, stretched out on the stones of Glam's grave. Every bone in his body was broken.

From then on, Glam's activities went from bad to worse and spread all along the valley. No one in any farm was safe. More of Thorhall's men were killed and so were many of his animals. In the end, everyone apart from Thorhall, his wife and a few loyal servants abandoned the farm for the winter and fled down to the coast. All the nearby farms were left deserted. Everyone in that part of Iceland lived in fear of their lives and no one had any idea what to do.

Chapter 4
The Strongest Man in Iceland

No one was more interested in the goings on in Shadow Vale than a man called Grettir Asmundarson. He was the strongest man living in the country, and a very great hero. Grettir was often heard to say that he could beat any three warriors in battle whenever he chose, and that four wouldn't be out of the question. He proved his words true several times over, for he was quick to protect his friends from arrogant neighbours and quicker still to repay any insult to his honour. He had killed many men in various disputes and people became very wary of taking him on.

No one dared say anything bad about Grettir, but some men shook their heads whenever his name came up. "He's a great fighter, all right," they muttered into their ale, "but is he lucky? He's not frightened of anything, and is too head-strong for his own good. He never knows when to stop and think things over. Every enemy he kills, he makes ten more, because all the dead man's relatives swear revenge. If he carries on like this, he'll soon have half of Iceland against him."

But Grettir didn't care. Nothing seemed too difficult for him and his worst problem was that he was often bored. He was eager for a real challenge that would test his strength.

It so happened that Grettir's uncle Jokul lived at the end of Shadow Vale, and Grettir went to visit him.

"Tell me," Grettir said, "are half the stories that I've been hearing really true? This Glam seems to have got everyone tied up in knots!"

"It's no laughing matter, nephew," Jokul replied. "This must be the worst haunting that I can remember. Glam is more wicked than any other ghost and if, as I suspect, you're thinking of poking your nose into the affair, take my advice – stay well away! This is a very different matter to bashing a few heads together."

"Maybe, but I might just call in on Shadow Vale anyway," Grettir said. "I've heard the scenery is good up there."

His uncle leaned forward and grasped Grettir's arm. "Listen," he said, "all our family has high hopes of you. We don't want to see you waste the gifts you've been born with. Believe me, if there's one sure way of bringing ill luck down on your head, it's tangling with evil spirits. Nothing good can come from them. Stay here with me for the winter. Many of my friends have very pretty daughters who are on the look-out for a man like you. We can visit them and see what you think."

Grettir shook his head. "I've no interest in chasing girls while our neighbours are being murdered," he said. "And nor should you. It could be your farm Glam visits next. Thank you for your offer, Uncle, but I will set off early tomorrow and see what Thorhall has to say for himself."

"Do what you must," Jokul said sadly. "I'll say no more."

Chapter 5
Staying the Night

The next day, Grettir rode up the valley to Thorhall's farm. When Thorhall saw Grettir, he went out to greet him.

"Where are you going?" he asked.

"I was wondering if I could stay with you tonight," Grettir said, getting down from his horse.

Thorhall looked surprised. "Of course, if you wish," he said, "but perhaps you don't know where this is. I wouldn't want you to suffer on my account, so I may as well tell you that both you and your horse are at risk if you remain here."

"A new horse is easily bought," said Grettir.

With this, Thorhall welcomed him to his farm. They led the horse into the stable, locked the door and went into the house. That night, everyone slept soundly. Glam did not appear.

In the morning, Thorhall went out to check the horse, but all was well. The farmer was pleased, but baffled. "I don't know how you did it," he said. "That's the first time we've been left alone for months."

"Maybe Glam's changed his ways," Grettir said. "Or maybe he hasn't. I think I might stay here another night, if you don't mind."

Thorhall was happy to agree. The day passed and night came. Everyone went to bed. In the morning nothing seemed to have happened, but when Thorhall and Grettir went out to the stable they found that the door had been broken in, the stalls smashed apart and the horse torn to pieces.

"What did I tell you?" Thorhall moaned. "We are cursed! It will never end! Well, my friend, you've lost your horse, but there's no need to lose your life as well. Set off on foot now. You'll be well away from this wretched place by twilight."

Grettir was looking at the remains of his horse. "I'm not going without payment for my loss," he said. "The least that ghost can do is give me a good look at him in return. No, I

shall stay here again tonight and see if I can meet him."

Thorhall didn't know whether to laugh or cry. "It is a great blessing that you are willing to stay and keep us company," he said, "but I warn you that no good has ever come from meeting Glam. Still, if that's what you want to do –"

Grettir slapped him on the back. "Let's go and get some breakfast," he said.

Chapter 6
Waiting for Glam

The farmer and Grettir spent the day talking together. Outside it slowly grew dark. At last everyone went to bed, apart from Grettir, who sat quietly in the middle of the room beside the dwindling fire.

He looked about him. There were plenty of signs in the house of past damage caused by Glam. The main door had been broken off its hinges and had been replaced with a simple board. One of the crossbeams above the door-way had been split almost in two.

All the people of Thorhall's household were tucked up in their beds. Everything was very quiet. A torch was burning on the wall. Grettir got up and went over to a sturdy bench facing the doorway. He lay down on it and covered himself from head to toe with a thick fur cloak. He arranged it so that he could peep out through a tiny gap in the fur, and kept his eyes fixed on the broken door.

The fire burned low, the room grew cold. Grettir began to shiver under the cloak. Once or twice he heard snores from Thorhall's bed, but otherwise it was very still. He watched the light flicker and dim.

All at once there was a loud clatter from outside, as if a metal-rimmed bucket had been kicked hard among the stones of the yard. Then there was a great thud as something heavy landed on the roof. Grettir listened hard. He heard slow, dragging footsteps climbing the roof to the centre beam, then a thunderous banging as something began to beat its heels furiously against the turf. Flakes of bark and dirt fell from the ceiling like heavy snow. The cracked beam above the door sagged a little more. The whole hall shook.

After a long while the banging stopped. Grettir listened to the slow, dragging footsteps climbing down the roof to the edge. There was a muffled impact as heavy feet landed on the ground, and then he heard them shuffling round towards the door of the house. Grettir remained very still under his cloak.

Something pushed against the door, and the stout beam that held it shut snapped like a twig. The door opened. In peered Glam's head, as big as that of an ox or a horse. The

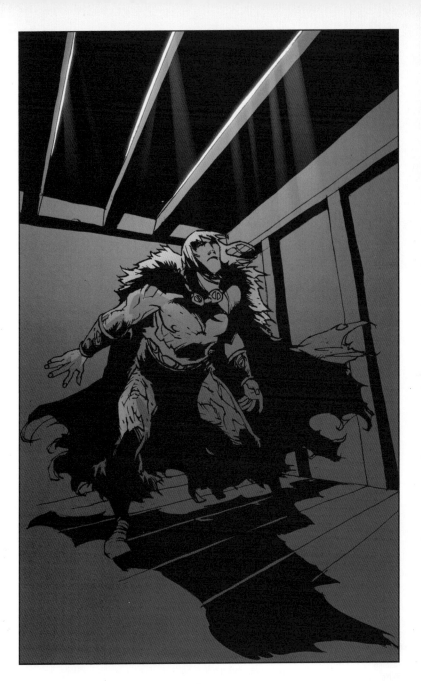

face was swollen to a colossal size, the skin mottled white and blue, the eyes staring from their sockets.

Slowly, Glam squeezed through the door into the hall. He was still wearing the tunic and leggings he had worn on the day he died, but they were ragged and torn, the pale flesh swelling through. Once inside, Glam stood upright. He was so tall that his streaked grey hair crackled against the rafters.

Glam moved his great heavy head from side to side, scanning the room. As he looked, he ground his teeth together, making a noise like a metal blade being dragged against a rock. He stretched out a huge hand to where the torch hung on the wall. His fingers cupped the end of the burning torch and snuffed the light out.

Now the room was dark, apart from a little moonlight shining in through the

doorway. Grettir could hardly see where Glam was. He felt a terrible urge to get up, to cry out and run, but he forced himself to remain as still as a stone under the cloak. In the blackness, he heard a slow movement, heard the scraping of Glam's teeth coming nearer and nearer. Grettir stayed dead still.

Two great eyes shone in the dark above him.

Chapter 7
The Fight

Glam saw the big bundle of furs lying on the bench. He bent down and reached out at them to pick them up. Grettir felt a grip like iron on the cloak. He pressed his feet against the side of the bench and made himself rigid, hanging on to the cloak from beneath it.

Glam pulled at the cloak. Nothing happened – the cloak stayed where it was. Glam pulled once more. Still the cloak didn't move. Grettir hung on with all his might, gritting his teeth with the effort. Glam tried again, and this time he wrenched at the cloak so hard that Grettir was dragged up off the bench and onto his feet.

The cloak ripped in two. Glam staggered back, and as he did so Grettir leapt forwards, ducked under the swinging arms and grabbed him around his waist. He tried to over-balance Glam so that he would fall. But Glam clutched at Grettir's arms in order to twist him loose, and in this way, locked together, they careered around the darkened hall, crashing into benches and splintering them to match-wood.

Grettir had never felt anything in his life as strong as the cold fingers now digging into his flesh. The terrible grip tightened, it began to force him downwards, hoping to crush him against the earth. Grettir's legs were buckling. He stumbled backwards towards the fire-place. Over the hearth-stones and

through the red-hot embers they went – Glam pushing, Grettir in retreat. Red sparks exploded up into the darkness from each impact of their scuffling feet.

Once beyond the fire-place, Grettir exerted all his strength. He braced his feet and twisted, swinging Glam round and slamming him hard into the roof post in the centre of the hall. The post split down the middle. One of the rafters fell, bringing with it pieces of turf. But Glam remained standing. The grip on Grettir's neck did not falter.

Without warning, Glam stepped backwards and began to pull Grettir towards the doorway, seeking to drag him outside. Grettir knew that if he was brought out into the open, Glam's power would overcome him. He tried to jam his feet against anything he passed – trestle-tables, posts or benches – but each time Glam pulled so hard that Grettir was forced forwards against his will.

Now Grettir was in desperate straits, for his strength was almost at an end. But he had one final trick to try. Just before they arrived at the doorway, when Glam was pulling him with all his might, he suddenly stopped resisting. Instead, he threw himself forwards, ramming against Glam's chest.

Taken by surprise, Glam toppled backwards, falling heavily against the beam above the door. The beam split in two and the roof burst open above it. Glam and Grettir crashed through the doorway in a shower of splintered wood and roof turf. Glam landed on a jagged rock with an impact that snapped his back in two. Grettir landed on Glam.

Then the moon broke out through a hole in the clouds. A beam of light bathed them, and Glam's eyes shone up at the moon full of wickedness and hate. At this sight, Grettir's knees turned to water, and the strength in

his arms ebbed away. He could not draw his sword, he could not move; he lay there upon the body of Glam, swallowed by a haze of fear.

As if in a dream, he heard the voice of Glam speaking to him.

"Well, Grettir," it said, "I cannot say I am pleased to have met you, but I shall make sure that you also regret meeting me. I have fallen, but I still have the power to curse you, and this I will do. Tonight you are strong, but you are only half as strong as you would have become if you had left me alone. Moreover, your strength, which has always brought you fame, will bring you nothing but ill luck from now on. I see you being forced away from the warmth of people's homes, to dwell by yourself in lonely places, a fugitive from men. And each night, while you cower alone in the darkness, you shall feel my eyes watching you, so that you are driven mad with terror. And this fear will kill you at the last."

At that moment, the moon went in behind a cloud. The light in Glam's eyes went out and his voice faded. Grettir felt the strength return to his limbs. He got up, drew his sword and cut off Glam's head.

Chapter 8
Victory?

Grettir heard a small noise behind him. Thorhall was peeping out of the shattered doorway. When he saw Grettir standing holding Glam's severed head, he came out with a vigorous step, loudly thanking God and praising Grettir for his victory.

Grettir said little, but ordered the farmer to prepare a great bonfire. That very night they burned Glam's body. As dawn broke, they swept the ashes up into a bag, which

they carried away and buried in a remote place. Then they returned to the farm. Grettir slept all day.

When news got out about the fight, Grettir's fame spread across all of Iceland. He was called the bravest man then living, and showered with gifts by the people of the district.

But Grettir didn't celebrate that much. When Thorhall offered him anything that he owned, Grettir said, "A new horse would be good. And maybe some new clothes. My ones are a bit torn." Beyond that, he was not much interested in his reward.

For the fact was that already some of Glam's words had come true. At night, Grettir didn't like being on his own. He saw shadows and shapes lurking on the edge of his vision, and felt that he was being watched.

And ever afterwards, though he slew robbers, killed trolls and giants, and did many other astonishing deeds, the curse of the ghost of Shadow Vale hung over Grettir Asmundarson. To the end of his life, the strongest man in Iceland remained afraid of the dark.

Jonathan Stroud

Author

Favourite hero:
Odysseus, from the Greek myths. He isn't the strongest guy around, but he's *clever*. And that means he survives.

Favourite monster:
Fenrir, from the Norse myths. He's big, he's bad, he's a wolf, and at the End of the World he swallows the king of the Gods. That's just about as nasty as a monster can get.

Favourite fight scene:
Beowulf against Grendel, in the poem *Beowulf*. The hero waits for the monster in a darkened hall, just like Grettir does with Glam. Perhaps the Icelandic poet knew the English poem, written a few hundred years before?

RELOADED

Siku

Illustrator

Favourite hero:
Batman – who else? Batman is for grown-ups, Spiderman is for kids and Superman is just a loser who wears red pants outside his blue suit ... give me a break!

Favourite monster:
Everyone loves King Kong – besides, he isn't slimy.

Your weapon of choice:
Telekinesis – moving things with my mind.

Favourite fight scene:
When Bruce Lee faces Chuck Norris in the film *Way of the Dragon*.

Goodie or baddie:
A goodie scaring the life out of bad bosses.

RELOADED

Barrington Stoke would like to thank all its readers for commenting on the manuscript before publication and in particular:

Seamus Bradley
Dara Brady
Jacqueline Brady
Nathaniel Evans
Alistair Fazakerley
Libby Fazakerley
Michael Fisher
Connlaoth Harkin
Nathan Harkin
Peter Higgins
John Hoey
Sean Melly
Chloe Middlehurst
Frazier Owen
Jill Parker
Dana Reeves
Stephanie Roberts
Dylan Stafford

Become a Consultant!

Would you like to give us feedback on our titles before they are published? Contact us at the email address below – we'd love to hear from you!

info@barringtonstoke.co.uk
www.barringtonstoke.co.uk

YOUNG MERLIN
BY
TONY BRADMAN

Merlin knows he's not like other boys.
He has nightmares every night and people laugh at him on the street.
But when the king's men come to take him away, he begins a journey that is beyond his wildest dreams ...

You can order *Young Merlin* directly from
www.barringtonstoke.co.uk

TAM O'SHANTER

BY
LARI DON

A scream shatters the moonlit night.

Tam has seen what no-one should see.

And they know it.

Hell has broken loose.

Fears you can't name. Nightmares come real.

And they are out to get him.

Can Tam outrun death?

You can order *Tam O'Shanter* directly from
www.barringtonstoke.co.uk

THE EVIL EYE
BY
OISIN McGANN

Fire. Ashes. Death.

This is what happens when Balor opens his

Evil Eye.

No-one can escape.

Lug has trained for years to fight this battle. But

can he save his people?

You can order *The Evil Eye* directly from
www.barringtonstoke.co.uk

WANTED: JANOSIK

BY
ANDREW MATTHEWS

Killer. Thief. Outlaw.

And he's the good guy ...

Hero to the poor. Hated by the rich.

Wanted: Janosik.

Dead Or Alive.